Varnell Roberts, Super-Pigeon

Varnell Roberts, Super-Pigeon

By Genevieve Gray

Illustrated by Marvin Friedman

Houghton Mifflin Company Boston 1975

Also by
GENEVIEVE GRAY
Sore Loser

Library of Congress Cataloging in Publication Data

Gray, Genevieve S
  Varnell Roberts, super-pigeon.

  SUMMARY: Seventh-grader Varnell Roberts is a
victim in a schoolyard shake-down racket until a
secret project in behavior modification helps him
turn the tables on his tormentors.
  [1. School stories. 2. Interpersonal rela-
tions] I. Friedman, Marvin. II. Title.
PZ7.G7774Var [Fic] 75-12576
ISBN 0-395-21408-4

w 10 9 8 7 6 5 4 3 2 1

To Paul and Hazel

Varnell Roberts, Super-Pigeon

one

To begin with, you have to understand that my troubles didn't automatically begin the minute I transferred to Rio Verde Junior High School. Far from it. My life has been screwed up ever since first grade for a couple of reasons, one being my size and the other being that people thought I was smarter than I was.

The problem about my size has been with me from birth when my mom had to cut all my diapers in half so they'd fit. But my reputation as a superbrain originated when I apparently said something erudite by mistake to Sister Theresa, my first grade teacher. She thereupon spread the word at St. Michael's that shrimpy little Varnell Roberts was a genius.

The reputation stuck even though it was a lie. I was not a genius then and am not a genius now but by second grade, Snooky Barent had already taught me how valuable it was if everyone thought so. Next to me, Snooky Barent was the littlest kid in class but whereas I was just average with a reputation for brains, Snooky was on the stupid side and everyone knew it. Kids teased him and rubbed dirt in his hair and if anything, the teachers were worse. From the way the teachers treated him, you'd have thought he didn't exist at all!

The lesson I learned from Snooky Barent was that if you were born a runt, it is better if everyone thinks you are smart. As long as everyone believes the myth, they will treat you like a person, not a freak, and that's all that counts.

All through elementary school, there were kids in my room smarter than I was and I had to be continually on my guard to keep it from showing. Al Herndon could work long division twice as fast as I could and his answers were always right. Every time. Not four out of five times, like mine. When it looked like Sister might call on me to go up against Al Herndon at the board working long division, I went to the bathroom. I did a lot of sneaky stuff like that. I had

2

more tricks up my sleeve than Richard M. Nixon.

It couldn't last and I knew it. Sixth grade was a nightmare. Some of the kids were growing taller by an inch a day, but not me. I hadn't even grown up to the big-kid desks in our room and had to sit with my legs dangling because my feet wouldn't reach the floor. Physically, I was arrested at the fourth grade level and since my mom is only five feet tall herself, full grown, I recognized the possibility that I might not grow any taller, ever.

Depressing as my physical dilemma was, my intellectual dilemma was worse. Lessons had gotten more complicated and it was harder than ever to maintain my image as a child wizard. And after sixth grade, I had St. Bartholomew's to look forward to, where kids won essay contests and the editors of the student newspaper were recognized as the best in the nation. Given a choice, I'd rather have sailed with Prince Valiant to quell the barbarian hordes than tilt with the scholars at St. Bartholomew's.

When Mom decided to send me to Rio Verde instead of parochial school, it was a reprieve, though not without qualification. Public school is easier than parochial school and there was less chance I'd encounter a squad of Al Herndons in every class. But at Rio

3

Verde Junior High, I might be done in, in another way. The meanest kids in town went there. The year before, the school had been broken into nine times and a teacher had gotten jumped after a ball game and beaten up so bad he ended up in the hospital. They had a cop on duty full time over there but he never caught anybody.

Mom knew all that, and she wouldn't have sent me to Rio Verde but she had to. At St. Bartholomew's, there was $500 tuition and I would have needed bus fare to ride back and forth across town every day. After Dad was killed in a car wreck when I was eight, Mom got a job as bookkeeper for this supermarket downtown. We had trouble as it was, living on her salary, so there really wasn't any choice about the school thing. Rio Verde was it. Period.

I went over to sign up one morning about the middle of August. Little dreaming what a waste of time it would turn out to be, I spent the last week of vacation studying the first chapters of all my textbooks. If possible, I intended to preserve my camouflage as a superbrain and win the respect of my new classmates.

For the first two days of classes, I got along pretty well. In math I successfully multiplied 27.5603 by 94.006 and in social studies I knew that the capital of

Chad was Fort Lamy. The school building was unfamiliar but I was lucky and didn't get lost, thank goodness. I could have blown my cover right there.

The third morning, matters took a turn for the worse. Much worse.

Rio Verde is about six blocks from my house but the main building faces on Prince Road. I walked to school every morning and came in the back way at the Florence Avenue gate. There were never any kids hanging around there, the Florence Avenue gate being about as far from the main building as you can get and still be on the school grounds.

This morning I am telling about, I saw three big guys coming across the school grounds toward me. Switchblade types, they were — one black, one a greasy blond, and a third character built like a sumo wrestler. I sensed trouble and looked for the cop who always prowled the school grounds before the first bell rang in the mornings. I spotted him, all right. He was over by the building, spruced and starched in his blue uniform, surrounded by a swarm of admiring females.

By that time the three guys had formed a semicircle and were gazing down at me in the middle as if I were some kind of curious insect. It was the blond who seemed to be the leader. His jeans clung to his legs

5

like scales on a lizard and the granny glasses he wore magnified his eyes to milky blue puddles.

"What's your name?" he said.

"Varnell Roberts."

The black guy laughed, only it was more like a whinny. "Little 'un, ain't he?"

The wrestler stood there with his hands on his hips, chewing a wad of gum. He didn't say a word. He didn't have to. The sheer size of him was enough to make you forget what you were about to say.

"How much money you got, Peewee?" the leader asked, jerking his head to get the hair out of his eyes.

"A quarter," I lied.

He signaled the wrestler, who grabbed my arms from behind. It was like being caught in a hydraulic press. When I tried to kick free, my wrist was slowly twisted till I could feel the bones grinding.

The other two quickly went through my pockets where they found not only my fifty cents for lunch but the two dollars to pay for a lab manual that Mr. Rodriguez had said we needed to buy for science.

The leader signaled the big guy to let me go, tucked the money in his pocket, jerked his hair out of his eyes again, and said, "You a new kid in school, else you wouldn't've lied like that. Won't get you nowhere."

He gathered a mouthful of spit and let fly at a nearby weed. He missed. "Rio Verde's a tough school," he said. "Little kids get hurt if they aren't careful. Oscar and Ernie and me, we got a protection club organized. Make sure won't nothing bad happen to little kids like you. This money you give us this morning, that's your initiation fee. You done joined the club."

"What if I don't want to join?" My voice came out in a thin squeak and they laughed.

"Dues is fifty cents, Peewee. Understand?" the leader went on, ignoring my protest. "Fifty cents. Every morning. We'll be here at the gate to meet you and collect."

He turned away, then paused and scratched his chest thoughtfully. "Last year we were taking care of a kid and he thought he knew a better way. Said he didn't want us protecting him. Tried talking it over with Mr. Podovsky. Kid's name was Clark. Billy Clark. Ask around. Get somebody to tell you what happened to Billy Clark."

They walked away then and I heard the wrestler suggesting they buy some peanuts at the snack bar before the bell rang. My money would be spent for snacks, apparently. I hoped they choked.

In spite of being warned against it, I didn't rule out

having a talk with Mr. Podovsky, at least not then. Mr. Podovsky was the principal of Rio Verde who handled the school discipline problems with the help of Mr. Miller, the assistant principal; Miss Nash, the dean of girls; and four counselors. (As I think I mentioned, there were a lot of discipline problems at Rio Verde Junior High School.)

In science class that morning, I told Mr. Rodriguez I'd have to bring my two dollars for the manual later. Going without lunch was harder. You wouldn't know it to look at me, but I am strongly addicted to food and the withdrawal pains that afternoon were something fierce — clammy palms, chills, and nausea.

Having been spared the necessity of eating lunch, I had time to kill at noon. I hunted up an eighth grader I knew who lived a couple of blocks from my house. He had been at Rio Verde the year before and I hoped he could tell me who my three new acquaintances were.

The eighth grader told me the big guy was Oscar Bridges and the black was Ernie Wilson. "Richard Hogarth is the mean one, though." He looked around nervously and lowered his voice. "Last year there was this girl he wanted to date but she told him to buzz off. Next day while classes were changing she was walking down the hall and felt someone brush against her. Next thing she knew, her arm was dripping blood. She'd been slashed with a razor."

I didn't believe him. "In the *hall?*" I scoffed. "Aw, c'mon!"

But he swore it was the truth. "Ask anybody. They'll tell you. You know how it is between bells — mobs of kids and you don't really see anyone. This girl was positive Richard did it but she never saw him and neither did anyone else."

I stared.

"Look," he went on nervously. "Stay away from that guy. He's worse than just mean, he's crazy."

"What about the cop?" I asked. "Can't the cop check up on him?"

"Old Everready? Sure, but what's to check? Richard never leaves a trace. Or if he does, he lies his way out of it and nobody ever pins anything on him."

"Do you know a kid named Billy Clark?" I asked.

"Billy Clark from last year? Yeah, he was in my homeroom. He's another one who got in trouble with Richard. The story went around that Richard and Ernie and Oscar did something to him, I don't know what. Billy Clark squealed to the cop and the cop went to Mr. Podovsky. All three of them ended up in juvenile court, only it was Billy Clark's word against theirs. Nobody could prove they'd done anything wrong."

"What homeroom is Billy Clark in this year? I'd like to talk to him."

"Not here at Rio Verde, you won't. He transferred to Warfield — for his health, I guess. Richard would've cut him to ribbons for getting him in trouble."

"You mean the school *let* Billy Clark transfer? If he lives in the Rio Verde district, doesn't he have to go to Rio Verde?"

"He doesn't live in the Rio Verde district anymore. His folks' house burned down. Some of the kids thought Richard Hogarth set it on fire but the fire department said there was a short in the wiring in the garage. Anyway, they moved. They'd have moved anyway, probably. At least, they would've if they had any sense."

The bell rang then and I got my books and went to English. Maybe having a talk with Mr. Podovsky wasn't such a hot idea.

two

When it came to law and order, I decided that animals in the zoo were more secure against unreasonable seizures than kids at Rio Verde Junior High School. It really shook me that a bandit like Richard Hogarth could operate a protection racket in school under the noses of a cop, the school brass, and the teachers and get off scot-free.

The more I thought about it, the harder it was to understand. Here was this extortionist who must have victimized plenty of kids besides Billy Clark and me. Why hadn't the others squawked?

The question barely hit me before I knew the answer. Only a few minutes before, I could have squawked to my eighth grade friend but didn't. Knowing I was a marked man would have scared him and he would have avoided me. There's a common belief that people go to bat for the underdog but try telling that to the Snooky Barents of this world. Underdogs are a big drag as I can attest, having thoroughly explored the territory of underdogdom on my own for the better part of my life.

In my case, at least, I knew I was right not to tell anyone — not the other kids, not Mr. Podovsky, and not Mom. Golly Pete — certainly not Mom! She'd have buzzed over to Mr. Podovsky's office to save me and next thing we'd have to pull a Billy Clark and move so I could transfer to another school. I knew I was better off to take it a day at a time and work it out myself.

A day at a time, I turned over my lunch money to Richard without any further argument. I didn't go hungry but my eating pattern changed. Mom and I always had our hot meals at noon and for supper we ate cornflakes or soup. We saved money that way, only now what I had instead of meat and vegetables at noon was a sandwich and maybe an apple or a pickle. The only reason I had that was because Mom left in the mornings before I did. She wasn't there to see me fixing a sandwich and to ask embarrassing questions about my cafeteria money which I was giving to Richard every day. Or almost every day. Three mornings he didn't show up. He never explained why and I didn't ask for fear he'd demand the back money he didn't collect.

Two weeks went by and I began to think I could go on indefinitely, sneaking lunches from home. In the cafeteria there was a long table reserved for kids who didn't go through the line but brought lunch from home. Boys sat at one end and girls at the other. The first few days I got the usual flak about my size. I spent one weekend memorizing the Dodgers' batting averages and Rose Bowl scores for the last ten years. After that, I became the group's handy pocket-sized reference work and kids stopped asking, "How's the weather down there?"

Just about the time I had my lunch arrangement worked out, it came to a halt. On Friday of the second week, Mom announced that one of the women in her office had left to have a baby and her hours had been changed because of it. She didn't have to go to work till 10 A.M. but had to stay later every day. Monday morning she was cleaning up the kitchen so I couldn't fix a sandwich.

Walking to school, I decided I'd better avoid the guys I'd gotten to know at lunch. They might ask too many questions. On the heels of that decision, I got to wondering why I was being so accommodating to Richard Hogarth anyway. Every morning he stuck out his hand and I dropped two quarters into it without a whimper. I decided I'd fight back for a change and try dodging him. If he wanted my money, let him hunt me up to collect.

I walked the extra three blocks around to the main school entrance on Prince Road instead of going in the Florence Avenue gate. The bell rang soon after that and I went to homeroom with my two quarters still snug in my pocket, happy as a cat full of chopped chicken liver. It was such a brilliant idea I was ashamed for not having thought of it before.

They hit me in third period gym class. When I came back to the locker room to shower and dress, all my clothes and books were gone. Shoes, socks, notebook, pencils, the lunch money in my pants pocket — everything.

When I realized how easy it had been for them, it made me a little sick. Every kid in every gym class was assigned a locker and the kids' names and locker numbers were listed alphabetically on the bulletin board at

one end of the locker room. All Richard had to do was get out of class long enough to come to the locker room while all the kids were out on the field, find my locker number on the bulletin board, give the cheap lock a sharp tug, and empty the locker.

I reported the theft to Coach. I knew it wouldn't do any good, and as far as catching up with Richard was concerned, it didn't. Coach loaned me an exercise suit so I could go home for clothes to finish out the day. On the way home, I suddenly remembered that my house-key had also been in my pants pocket along with the money and had been stolen with everything else. Mom had always left a housekey with our next-door neighbor in case of my ever getting locked out, but that wasn't the problem. The problem was that now Richard Hogarth had a key to our house. He could ditch school and come ransack the house while both Mom and I were gone or he could sneak in at night while we were asleep. I didn't like it.

That afternoon when I told Mom I got ripped off, she was furious. "What kind of a snake would do a thing like that? Don't you have any idea who took your things?"

"No," I lied.

"What's Mr. Podovsky going to do about it? What about that cop they have over there?"

"Coach took down a list of my stuff that got swiped. But —"

"But what?"

I tried to explain. "Mom, it could've been anybody in school."

"You're trying to tell me they aren't going to do anything at all about it. Is that it?"

I shrugged.

She fumed some more and said she was going to telephone Mr. Podovsky next morning and ask him why he allowed lawless elements to operate in his school. I wondered too.

Before dark that afternoon, I knocked on a few doors around the neighborhood and finally lined up a lady who would let me come do her yard work every weekend for a dollar. The next morning I went through the Florence Street gate and paid the toll as usual.

"Heard you had some trouble yesterday," said Richard sociably.

When I didn't answer, Ernie giggled. "Peewee got on a sweater today. What happen to your nice jacket, Peewee?"

The sweater I had on was mended in a couple of

places and a button was missing but it was all I had left to wear.

Richard said to me, "I warned you, remember? Remember I told you what a tough school we got here? Pay you to keep up your dues, not fall behind anymore."

Later that morning, Coach said, "Is this your math book?" He'd found it in his wastebasket the afternoon before. He and Mr. Podovsky had alerted the janitors and sure enough, stuff of mine turned up in litter cans all over school. Eventually I got back my math and science books, my pants, shirt, underwear, and one shoe with a sock in it. But that was all. My pants pockets were empty, naturally, and my notebook never turned up and neither did my windbreaker or the other shoe.

And neither did my housekey.

Looking back, my chest knots up just thinking about the way things were then. At the beginning of school, I'd worried about impressing people with my nonexistent genius but compared to the hassling I'd gotten from Richard, a little thing like classroom status seemed pretty trivial. There wasn't a minute of the day when I wasn't either boiling with resentment over what Richard and Ernie and Oscar were doing to me or

19

cold with fear of what they might think up to do if they happened to be in a playful mood. I couldn't concentrate in class, forgot to do homework assignments, and was making the worst grades I'd ever made in my life. I'd turned into a loner, avoiding even the kids I knew from my neighborhood.

My first week's earnings from doing yard work went to help buy new shoes. I was going without lunch nearly every day and getting more desperate by the hour.

At the beginning of school, I'd been assigned to Miss Karl's homeroom. One day Miss Karl gave me some money she'd collected for the girls' cheerleader costumes and told me to take it to the office. The secretary in the office counted it and said there was a dollar too much. She gave me the dollar to take back to Miss Karl.

My judgment was addled from hunger or I wouldn't have tried what I did. I decided to wait until the next day to give back the dollar to Miss Karl and in the meantime I'd borrow fifty cents of it to eat lunch that day. To replace the fifty cents, I dreamed up a scenario so juvenile I'm ashamed to tell it.

I planned to tell Mom I lost a tooth. I even had the tooth to show her — an old one I'd saved in my sock drawer. I would then kid Mom into putting fifty cents under my pillow the way she used to when I was a little kid and believed in the Tooth Fairy.

(I warned you it was juvenile.)

It wasn't till I got home that afternoon and got out my old tooth that I realized there was a flaw in the plan. The reason I had saved the tooth was because it marked an occasion. It was my last baby tooth which I had lost the year before. Mom would understandably be somewhat skeptical if not downright worried and would most likely ask to see the empty space in my mouth where the tooth had been. But the empty spaces in my mouth were all filled up with perfectly good permanent teeth. I got out the pliers and tested every tooth in my head trying to find a loose one I could pull so I could qualify for my fifty cents, but no luck.

I abandoned the plan.

Next day at school I had a sore neck from trying to pull my teeth but no money to replace the fifty cents I had embezzled. The office secretary had already told Miss Karl about it by the time I got to homeroom. When I produced only half the money, Miss Karl sent me to Mr. Podovsky's office.

Going down the hall, all I could think of was Mom and her phone conversation with Mr. Podovsky after my clothes got swiped in gym class. I didn't think Mr. Podovsky knew who I was and I hoped he wouldn't connect me up with the irate lady who phoned him. I had a hunch that such a sudden switch from victim to culprit wouldn't win me any Brownie points.

In case I haven't said so before, Mr. Podovsky is the principal of Rio Verde Junior High School. He looks like Telly Savalas with hair. He bites off the ends of his words and looks at you with a piercing glare calculated to liberate your innermost thoughts. He scared the bejesus out of me.

I stood inside his office door like a whipped dog waiting for a boot in the gut.

"Why did you take the money when you knew it wasn't yours?" he asked me.

"I was hungry," I mumbled.

"Speak up. What did you do with the money?"

"Bought lunch with it."

"Don't your folks give you money for lunch?"

"Sometimes," I lied.

Mr. Podovsky drew a deep breath. "I'll have to phone your mother."

"Mom's at work. Her boss gets mad if she gets phone calls at work. She'd get in trouble." That much was true.

"What about your father?"

It was the last question I expected and it knocked the breath out of me. "He's dead," I whispered.

There was a pause. "You'll have to bring the money from home tomorrow to replace what you took."

"We haven't —" The question about Dad had shaken me up so, I was about to bawl. I hated it but I couldn't help it. I tried again, "Mom doesn't have enough money —" I bit my lip, then, and blinked hard at the floor.

When Mr. Podovsky finally spoke, his voice was softer. "Maybe you could work it out here at school. I'll send you down to Mrs. Bowker in the cafeteria."

When I reported to Mrs. Bowker, one of her kitchen helpers was taking some big pans of peach cobbler out of the oven. They smelled and looked so delicious, I couldn't concentrate on Mrs. Bowker's instructions. She took pity on me and ladled up a big dish for me before I went to work. I consumed it with such relish she beamed with pride.

To work out the money I owed, Mrs. Bowker made me fill and tidy up the mustard and ketchup bottles. Next, I filled all of the paper napkin holders and wiped out the lunch trays. I worked like a rookie Scout earning his first merit badge and as I hoped, she had another sustainer waiting for me when I finished — a fresh taco to eat on the way back to class.

As I was about to leave, I said, "Mrs. Bowker, why can't I come help you again sometime? Without being sent by Mr. Podovsky, I mean."

"That would be nice, wouldn't it?" she said, patting me on the shoulder. "If it weren't against the rules, I'd have you here every day. You're a good worker, Varnell."

Some consolation.

The rest of that day, I kept mulling over the curious fact that Mr. Podovsky didn't recognize my name even though Mom had phoned him about me only a couple of weeks before. I was forced to conclude that at Rio Verde Junior High School, student misdeeds were so common that without a program, Mr. Podovsky couldn't keep up with the players.

If he didn't recognize me once, maybe he wouldn't recognize me twice. I began to think in terms of another transgression that would get me sent to the cafeteria. It had to be minor enough to fade quickly from Mr. Podovsky's memory bank but still serious enough to warrant punishment.

For two more days after that, I went without lunch but the third day I went to the library, got the latest copy of *National Geographic* from the magazine rack, and sat down at a table in front of the librarian's check-out desk where I proceeded to tear out all the interesting pictures. When I was sent to confront Mr. Podovsky in his office, he again sent me to the cafeteria without remembering that I was a repeater.

At the time I vandalized the *National Geographic*, I was aware that two wrongs don't make a right. Still, my wrong against the school — which I paid for — seemed minor in relation to Richard's wrong against me — which he hadn't so much as received a slap on the wrist for. Somehow I didn't feel guilty.

A few days after the *National Geographic* episode, I busted open a vending machine. Again Mr. Podovsky sent me to the cafeteria. Mrs. Bowker and I were becoming good friends. She was getting so she really depended on me.

It wasn't till four or five offenses later that Mr. Podovsky learned my name and the jig was up. I was sent to the office for swiping chalk out of Mr. Rodriguez's supply closet.

"I'm sending you to the cafeteria again," Mr. Podovsky said, writing on a notepad. "Also, I'm transferring you from Miss Karl's homeroom to the special ed room."

I have to explain about the special ed room. At St. Michael's, we'd never had anything called special education so the whole operation was a big mystery when I first heard about it at Rio Verde. Special ed students were crippled or retarded kids, I found out. They had a few of their classes like art and shop with the regular students but most of their classes were in separate rooms with separate teachers in a separate wing of the building.

It was a long time before anyone explained to me that there was another special ed classroom down there with kids who weren't crippled or retarded. These kids were ornery. When the regular kids or the regular teachers talked about "the special ed room," they didn't mean the crippled kids, they meant the ornery kids. The special ed room was a kind of part-time school jail with seventh, eighth, and ninth grade kids incarcerated together and an ex-marine for a warden. When enough teachers got mad at a student, they sentenced him to the special ed room for the duration. Or at least I never heard of anyone getting out. They just got in. The inmates were all supposed to be incorrigible, meaning there was no hope for them, ever, and they were expected to graduate from the special ed room straight into the state penitentiary.

Since I had never thought of my irregular behavior as criminal but more in the line of survival, the last thing that occurred to me was that I might be a candidate for the special ed room.

As soon as the initial shock wore off, I thought of Mom and what she'd say when she found out where I'd been sent and why. Mr. Podovsky didn't say anything about notifying her. I offered up a silent prayer that he wouldn't.

I checked out of Miss Karl's homeroom not knowing exactly what I was in for. I went down the hall to the special ed wing and presented myself to Mr. Jarrett, the ex-marine with the stainless steel personality who ran the room for incorrigibles. I stood in front of Mr. Jarrett's desk while he explained crisply that four of my classes would be the regular ones I always went to, but I would spend the other three periods every day with my fellow convicts.

While he was signing me in, I glanced around the classroom and froze. Three of my new classmates were already known to me. They were Richard Hogarth, Ernie Wilson, and Oscar Bridges.

Mr. Jarrett was explaining something and I tried to pay attention. "You'll be on a different schedule now," he was saying. "Special ed classes have a different lunch period. Also, all classes in this wing begin fifteen minutes earlier every morning and let out fifteen minutes earlier every afternoon than the rest of the school. Be sure you aren't tardy in the morning."

A different lunch period? I'd wondered why I'd never seen Richard or Ernie or Oscar on the school grounds at noon and had concluded they were out shoplifting somewhere. But *fifteen minutes earlier every morning?* I had to ask Mr. Jarrett to repeat it and even then I had trouble believing what it meant. All those mornings I'd been turning over my lunch money to Richard, he'd been going in the building to class fifteen minutes earlier than I did. That explained why he and Ernie and Oscar missed some mornings but not others. All those times they were collecting my lunch money, I could have dodged them simply by coming to school a few minutes later in the morning and hanging around school in the afternoon till I was sure they'd gotten tired and gone home.

If I'd had a rope, I would have hung myself.

three

Mr. Podovsky didn't phone Mom, he wrote her a letter. It was waiting in the mailbox when I got home from school next day. I looked at it a long time, wracking my brains to think of a way I could *not* open it. But there wasn't any way. I was in too deep.

"Dear Mrs. Roberts," it said. "It is imperative that you come to school for a conference about your son, Varnell. His records from St. Michael's show he was an outstanding student there, both in terms of scholarship and school citizenship, but he has failed to maintain this record at Rio Verde. It has become necessary for me to transfer him to a special class for problem students. Please telephone me at your earliest convenience for an appointment to discuss your son's failure to adjust to his new surroundings. Sincerely yours, Michael Podovsky, Principal."

I finally worked out a reply that said as little as possible. "Dear Mr. Podovsky. Varnell and I have had a talk about his trouble. Varnell has promised there will be no more stealing or vandalism. Yours truly, Marilyn Roberts."

I messed up five sheets of paper before I got a decent copy typed on Mom's old Remington and after that I practiced a long time before I had her signature right. I addressed the envelope and stamped it, then took it to the mailbox on the corner.

On the way back home, I reflected that to insure Richard Hogarth the pleasure of jingling a few coins in his pocket every day, I had undertaken a remarkable life of crime for one so young. In the month since I had fallen into his clutches, I had failed to report a crime, embezzled and stolen money and school supplies, defaced school property, tampered with the U.S. mail, and committed a forgery.

The day I was transferred to Mr. Jarrett's room at school, it was as if the door of a dungeon slammed shut behind me. Now that I was on the same schedule as Richard and Ernie and Oscar, they never missed a morning collecting. My yard work job paid a dollar the first weekend but less after that and some weekends nothing. Mom was seeing me off to school every morning and it was impossible to sneak anything out of the house to eat. At school, I was afraid to risk getting caught stealing. If I got caught again, Mr. Podovsky and Mom were certain to make contact and gang up on me.

I was afraid to ditch school or pretend to be sick and stay at home for the same reason — I might get caught, plus if Richard got the idea I was deliberately avoiding him again, there was no telling what lousy trick he might dream up. What worried me most was that I might really get sick. I was getting thinner and thinner from going without lunch so often. My gut ached all the time and I knew it wasn't unheard-of for kids my age to come down with stomach ulcers, especially if they were the kind that worried a lot. And I was worrying a lot.

It was weird being in the same class with Richard and Ernie and Oscar and it was especially weird being in the same class with eighth and ninth graders. We had English and social studies together except the seventh, eighth, and ninth grade kids sat together in different parts of the room. Also we had a supervised study period together and supervised games and recreation on the school grounds at noon. I found out Oscar Bridges was as poorly coordinated as an elk on stilts and Richard was a bird-boned weakling who couldn't make out the lettering on a twenty-foot billboard without his glasses. Oscar was the only one in the room learning spelling out of a third grade textbook. At least Richard and Ernie were labeled standard ninth graders, not remedial ninth graders like Oscar, but they weren't much better in the brains department.

When I realized what diddleheads they were, it made me madder than ever. Being swindled out of my lunch every day by sharp operators was bad enough, but to be conned by these clowns was more than I could take. I wasn't on good terms with any of my teachers, but I kept pestering them anyway about getting out of Mr. Jarrett's room. I longed for the return of the good old days when they missed collecting from me every now and then by accident.

And then one afternoon — it must have been about three weeks later — I was so hollow-eyed hungry I tried to swipe some locker money out of Coach's desk. I got caught. I never laid a finger on the money but I jammed the lock on Coach's desk drawer trying to pick it and ended up getting sent to the office anyway. (That gives you an idea of the way my luck was running about that time.)

It was while I was in the office waiting to get worked over by Mr. Podovsky that I heard Miss Cota trying to talk him into letting her do this experiment. There were some other kids waiting ahead of me, but I had a feeling I was in for a special session this time. There was enough hydrochloric acid churning around in my stomach to eat a hole in an army boot and I took a seat by the door, hoping I would get in first and get it over with.

The door to Mr. Podovsky's office wasn't exactly soundproof and even if it had been, Miss Cota had the kind of voice that could carry through the walls of Grant's Tomb. Miss Cota was director of special education programs for the whole school district and was in and out of the special ed wing at Rio Verde a lot. Everybody liked her. She was big and chesty with smile wrinkles, a moustache, and a very determined manner.

I heard her tell Mr. Podovsky she'd okayed the project with Mr. Wheeler, the superintendent. She said it was all set up, ready to go.

"Nope," said Mr. Podovsky. "Sorry."

"Why not?" Miss Cota demanded.

"It's controversial. Worse than that, it's degrading. Subjecting teachers to treatment like that — who ever heard of such a thing! These techniques have been used mainly on prison inmates and mental patients. And sure, they've worked wonders. But when you propose having Rio Verde students use them on their teachers, no dice. I won't be a party to such sneaky business."

"Why is it sneaky?" Miss Cota asked. "Your teachers know behavior modification techniques backwards and forwards. Conditioning, reinforcement — they know about Skinner and his pigeons, Pavlov and his dogs. All that stuff's included in their teacher training. It isn't as though they were defenseless victims!" There was a pause and she went on. "From a scheduling standpoint, it will be simple. There won't be extra paperwork for Mr. Jarrett or the office."

Mr. Jarrett? I listened harder.

"Look, Mike," Miss Cota continued. "Three years ago you asked me to set up a class here at Rio Verde for the tough kids your teachers couldn't control in regular classes. 'Incorrigibles' — that's what you called them. I didn't want to do it, remember? But I did. We set up the class and right away your teachers had a place to dump kids they didn't want. Let a kid smart off, the teacher labeled him incorrigible and sent him to the special ed room." Her voice rose. "Mike, those kids aren't incorrigible! You baby your teachers! They don't even try!"

"Sure they try!" Mr. Podovsky protested angrily. "My teachers are professional people! This is a tough school we have over here!"

"Okay, so you're in a tough part of town. Everyone grants that. Three years ago, Rio Verde had twice as many hard-core discipline problems as any other school in town — four percent." Her voice hardened. "But since then, Mike, you've shot up from four percent to *ten percent* —"

Mr. Podovsky tried to interrupt but she shouted him down. "You want me to believe *ten percent* of your students here at Rio Verde are incorrigible? Who're you kidding?"

Mr. Podovsky said something I couldn't hear.

"Where's it going to end?" Miss Cota asked. "Next year fifteen percent? Year after that — ?"

"Okay!" Mr. Podovsky roared. It was the cry of a beaten man.

Their voices sank to a murmur and then became audible again as they moved toward the door. Mr.

Podovsky said, "Five kids seem like such a drop in the bucket. Is five kids all you want?"

Then Miss Cota named the ones she wanted to be in her project. "Oscar Bridges, Richard Hogarth, Varnell Roberts, Levon Williams, and Ernie Wilson," she said.

When Mr. Podovsky opened his door, I was gripping the arms of my chair trying to keep my insides organized. Miss Cota slapped him on the shoulder in a burst of good will and sailed out. Mr. Podovsky looked down, saw me sitting there, and told me to come in.

I got his leftover irritation at being yelled down by Miss Cota, plus his anger at me because "you promised your mother you'd knock off this foolishness! Well, didn't you? What's she going to say when I tell her what you've done?"

With no warning, my stomach knotted and heaved. I clapped my hand over my mouth but Mr. Podovsky reacted even more quickly than I did. He was around his desk in a split second and suddenly I was flying through the air. Next thing, I was staring into the bowl of the john in his private washroom, wretching like a poisoned cat, and Mr. Podovsky was holding my

36

head to make sure I didn't miss and mess up his im-maculate, snow-white tiled floor.

"Damn!" I heard him murmur under his breath. I guess he was fed up with my juvenile reactions. The first time in his office I'd nearly bawled and this time I nearly threw up — because in spite of the dramatic prologue, I didn't. It was 2:30 in the afternoon and I hadn't eaten since 7:00 that morning. All I did was heave, but I did a lot of that.

He let me go, finally, but I was so weak that instead of straightening up as we both expected, my knees buckled and I slid to the floor.

"You didn't eat any lunch!" he accused.

I shook my head.

He started to say something else but there was a troubled look on his face. He helped me to a chair in his office, then gazed out the window, thinking.

"You haven't told your mother you're in Mr. Jar-rett's room, have you?" he said.

I shook my head.

He phoned Mrs. Bowker then, and told her to ex-pect me next day in the cafeteria. He said I was to work out the cost of the lock on Coach's desk which I had busted.

After he hung up, I felt better. Somehow I knew he wasn't going to tell Mom. I said, "Mr. Podovsky, how can I get out of the special ed room? Maybe if I could get back in regular classes, I wouldn't all the time be getting into trouble."

"You mean if you got away from the evil influences in the special ed room, you'd straighten out?" he asked through a mirthless smile. "That's a cop-out and you know it. If you want out of the special ed room, quit stealing." He stood and moved to the door. "Come on. I'm going to have the nurse drive you home."

It was a good thing. I was so weak I wasn't sure I could have made it on my own.

Mrs. Bowker was glad to see me next day. She said she'd missed me and gave me a tuna fish sandwich to prove it. After I finished my work, she gave me a handful of potato chips to eat on my way back to class. As luck would have it, I ran into Mrs. Tatum in the hall.

I have to tell you about Mrs. Tatum. Mrs. Tatum is the ninth grade science teacher. She is pretty enough to be on the front of a magazine and her husband is rich. Nobody knows what she's doing teaching school unless it's because she likes to boss people around and there are more people to boss around in a school than most other places. It wasn't any of her business what

I was doing in the hall but she made it her business anyway, as usual.

She accused me of stealing the potato chips I was eating and told me it was against the rules to eat in the hall. (It wasn't.) Then after a few parting insults, she ordered me to go where I was headed in the first place, to Mr. Jarrett's room.

When I got there, though, Mr. Jarrett said I'd been assigned to a "study group" that was meeting with Miss Cota in a room down the hall.

I braced myself, walked down the hall, and opened the door.

"Come in, Varnell," Miss Cota said.

She was sitting with the others at a table at the far end of the room. The student desks were pushed against the wall and in the middle of the floor stood a TV set and something on a tripod that I supposed was a TV camera. I hadn't heard Miss Cota say anything to Mr. Podovsky about any TV equipment and I wondered what it was doing there.

"You're in the right place," Miss Cota encouraged me. "Come have a seat."

Richard and Ernie were surprised to see me. Ernie turned up his nose and made a face. Richard frowned and said, "Peewee going to be in on this too?"

"Varnell?" said Miss Cota. "Sure he is. Any objections?"

"He ain't nothing but a cruddy little seventh grader," Richard said. "What's a dumb kid like him doing in here?"

"Varnell's grades are better than yours, mister," Miss Cota warned with a glare. "If that's dumb, what's with you?"

"But Varnell ain't nothing but a little kid," Richard protested.

"Let me worry about that," said Miss Cota. She told me again to sit down and I pulled up a chair between Levon and Ernie.

Levon Williams was a big black girl with a nose like a shovel and hair braided in six ratty pigtails with rubber bands on the ends. I'd gotten to know her in Mr. Jarrett's room where she'd been sent last year after she cut up the gym teacher for calling her a lumpheaded pickaninny. Levon usually ignored me, but I liked her. In her classes she acted like a real dingbat, even to the point of claiming she couldn't read or write. She could, and everybody knew it. All she wanted was easy books to read and she got what she wanted.

Miss Cota announced that the five of us were going to do "a formal experiment in the scientific modification of human behavior." It was a mouthful and Ernie had to clown around.

"Mama, them words is too long for *me!*" and he got up as if to make his escape.

"I'm not your mama," Miss Cota said, very firmly. "Sit down."

Ernie sat down.

Then she started to tell us about Project Behavior Mod. That's what the name of this experiment was — "Project Behavior Mod." "You'll meet here with me one hour every day," she said. "The rest of the time, every period but this one, you'll be in your other classes, but you'll be modifying — that means changing — the behavior of your teachers. Right now, teacher behavior toward you is negative, right? Antagonistic? You're going to change that behavior. We're going to show by this experiment that your teachers can be brought — by you — to behave toward you in a friendly, supportive way."

Richard gulped. "Whaa-aa-aa-aat," he said, starting high and ending low.

"This I got to see," Levon murmured, deadpan.

Miss Cota went on. "To do this, you need special training. That's what we'll be using the TV equipment for, your training program. You'll be keeping records, making daily reports, evaluating what you're doing, finding ways to do it better. At the end of the seven weeks of the project, if everything goes the way it's supposed to, your days of being considered problem students will be over." She beamed at us and continued. "I chose you partly because you represent a cross section of Mr. Jarrett's room and partly because I thought each of you had a good chance of succeeding. This doesn't mean you have to participate. You can back out now and I'll get someone else to replace you."

It was what I'd been hoping to hear. I pushed my chair back to leave.

"But get this, every one of you," Miss Cota went on. "If you decide to stay, two rules. One: You do as I say. No backsliding. No whining around that you forgot or you lost your temper or you aren't in the mood. Goof off and out you go."

Ernie rolled his eyes and groaned.

"Two:" said Miss Cota. "No one outside this group is to know what we're doing. No one is even to hear the words 'Project Behavior Mod.' After the project's over, then we'll tell everyone. But right now, nothing. Got that? Okay, now's the time to make up your minds. What do you say?"

Just as I started to speak up, Levon shrugged elaborately. "Might as well stay, I guess. Ain't got nothing better to do."

Ernie said he'd stay too. Then Richard and Oscar nodded.

That left me the only one getting out, which was keen with me even though I was sorry to walk away from the TV equipment. It looked like fun. I wondered what Miss Cota was going to use it for. I decided to wait till later to tell her I wouldn't be staying.

Miss Cota asked us about specific problems we had in class with our teachers. She took notes. Then as I hoped she would, she showed us how the TV equipment worked. It was neat. She trained the camera on us and we could see the picture the camera was taking on the monitor. It was like a mirror, only better because in a mirror you only see yourself full face, head on. By moving the camera around, Miss Cota let us see what we looked like from all angles.

At the end of the hour after the others left, I asked Miss Cota to get someone else to replace me.

She was nice about it. "Mind telling me why you want out?" she asked.

"I just think I'd be better off." While I had her, I asked, "Miss Cota, how can I get out of the special ed room? I wouldn't ask you if it wasn't important."

"That's what Project Behavior Mod is all about, Varnell — to get all five of you back into regular classes. If the project is a success, we'll train another group and transfer them too. And then another group and another. You've already been chosen for the first group. So if what you want is to get back in regular classes, why not stay where you are?"

I could hardly explain to her that what I really needed was to get on a different schedule from Richard and Ernie and Oscar. It was depressing.

I mumbled something about going to my next class and turned to go. "Thanks, anyway."

"You want to be transferred to regular classes *now?*" she asked. "Is that it?"

I nodded.

"Varnell, with teachers feeling about you the way they do right now, they wouldn't agree to have you back in their regular classrooms. Not even if Mr. Podovsky gave his okay. He told me this morning that Coach caught you trying to steal some money."

I hated having her know about it. I nodded again.

She sighed. "Are you sure you've made up your mind? You want me to find a replacement for you?"

"Yes."

On my way to the door, I passed the TV equipment.

Miss Cota had left the power on and I caught sight of myself on the monitor. When she had turned the camera on us before, we were all sitting at the table together and all I saw of myself was a blob.

What I saw now, alone on the screen, made me think of those pictures you see of Vietnam orphans with haunted eyes. With a shock, I realized I was looking at myself! *That was me!* At St. Michael's, I'd gone around looking like a kid out of the Sears catalog to protect my reputation. I knew I'd changed since then, but — !

I pulled up my pants and brushed the hair out of my eyes before I remembered Miss Cota was still there. But if she noticed me primping before the camera, she didn't say anything. She was busy packing her briefcase and putting on her coat. I had a fleeting suspicion that she chose the five of us from Mr. Jarrett's room not for the reasons she said but because we were the specimens who obviously needed help the worst.

I was halfway down the hall before I changed my mind. I went back and told Miss Cota I'd be there with the others the next day.

four

We called it "Miss Cota's class," and the thing I liked best about it that first day was that Richard didn't meet me at the Florence Avenue gate. I ate lunch with my fifty cents and tried not to read any good omens into it. I'd gotten my hopes up too many times before.

Kids in Mr. Jarrett's room thought Miss Cota was teaching us remedial reading and we didn't say if she was or wasn't. If she'd wanted to, she could have taught anything. She was the best teacher I ever had. All the time she was telling us stuff she wanted us to learn, she was asking us questions or having us repeat after her. There wasn't any way your mind could wander.

47

She started the first day of the project by explaining what behavior modification was. Richard had said, "Miss Cota, we're not going to change them teachers none. They got it in for us."

"How do you know?" Miss Cota asked.

"How do I know?" Richard repeated. " 'Cause of the way they act!"

"You can change the way people act," Miss Cota said. "That's what this project is all about. You do it by a technique called *re-in-for-cing*. You'll be using that word a lot. Say it."

Oscar and Levon were the only ones who repeated it with her. Miss Cota's black eyes flashed. "Everybody! Participate or else! Again!"

We all said it.

"What's reinforcing?" Miss Cota went on. "All right, let's suppose Oscar helps Levon lift a heavy box. Levon appreciates it. She says to Oscar, 'Oscar, I like you when you help me out like that.' Oscar, suppose that really happened and Levon really said that to you. Next time she needed your help with something, which would you be more likely to do, help her or walk away?"

"Help her," said Oscar.

"You see," Miss Cota explained, "when Levon says

that to Oscar, she rewards him. She makes him feel good. She *re-in-for-ces* his behavior so he'll be more likely to repeat it. Now let's take some examples with teachers. Richard, you have Mrs. Tatum for science. Tell us about a time she said something nice to you."

Richard's lip curled. "That old witch ain't never in her life said anything nice to me!"

"Did so," Levon said. "This morning she told you your test paper was better'n the one you did last week."

"See?" said Richard. "I ain't never gonna do nothing to suit that old lady. Finds fault with everything I do. Pick, pick, pick!"

"What d'you mean, 'pick, pick, pick'!" snapped Miss Cota. "She told you your work *improved!* She said something nice, mister. Can't you tell the difference between encouragement and a put-down? What did you say back to her?"

Richard wouldn't tell her so Levon did. "Richard told her to shove it."

Miss Cota looked at Richard in disgust. "Okay, wise guy, see what you did? Mrs. Tatum made a positive contact with you. She tried to tell you something good about your work. If she'd been rewarded for that behavior — if you'd said something nice to her —

she might have been inclined to repeat it. But no. Just the opposite."

Ernie asked, "What should he have said?"

"He could have said, 'Thank you, Mrs. Tatum. It's easier for me to learn when I know I'm improving.'"

Richard protested, "You got to be soft in the head if you think I could say something like that and have that old lady believe me!"

"She'll believe you if you mean it," said Miss Cota. "You've got to believe it yourself, down deep."

Richard tossed his head impatiently.

"Listen!" Miss Cota went on. "Did I say this job was going to be easy?" She surveyed the rest of us around the table. "Did I? Anybody?"

She let us think about it a minute. It definitely wasn't going to be easy to say nice things to a teacher like Mrs. Tatum and mean it.

Levon broke the silence. "Miss Cota, look to me like all you want to do is teach us to butter up the teachers. Apple-polishing. Don't take any scientific experiment to do that. Them rich kids does it all the time."

"Of course they do, but *what* you say to the teacher is only part of it," Miss Cota told Levon. "*When* you say it — that's where the science part of it comes in.

Every time one of your teachers initiates a positive contact, it has to be reinforced immediately. Right then."

She made us all say "positive contact" and explained what it was. It could be a statement of approval or a pat on the back.

"Or maybe if the teacher takes up for you?" asked Levon.

Miss Cota nodded.

"Or does you a favor?" said Ernie.

"You're catching on," said Miss Cota. "Any time the teacher makes a positive contact with you, *that's* the behavior you want to reward so the teacher will repeat it later."

It all began to sound familiar. At St. Michael's, we'd had one of those laboratories with folders to read and question-and-answer cards, all packed in a box. One of the folders I read told about this guy who taught a hen to dance by feeding her a grain of corn every time she moved her feet the way he wanted her to. I couldn't believe Miss Cota was showing us how to train our teachers like that guy trained his hen but I decided to ask anyway.

She didn't have a chance to answer because Richard butted in.

"Listen to Peewee!" he sneered. "Who asked you?"

It seemed to me Miss Cota took longer squelching Richard than was absolutely necessary. Afterwards, she glanced at her watch and announced that it was time to make our record sheets to use the next day. I had the impression she was relieved to have an excuse to change the subject. Maybe it was embarrassing.

That first week, Richard and Ernie and Oscar only collected money from me two mornings and I thanked my lucky stars I'd changed my mind and decided to stay with the project. Why they slowed down was something I couldn't figure out. Miss Cota was a very sharp teacher who didn't miss much and it might have been they were afraid their protection racket would leak out whether I intended for it to or not. Anyway if I had any doubts about staying in the project before, I didn't once it got started.

According to the schedule Miss Cota set up for us, the project would take seven weeks to complete, ending just before Christmas. We wouldn't do anything for the first two weeks but count positive and negative contacts. We each had a record sheet we kept in the backs of our notebooks with our teachers' names in a column down the left side. To the right of the teachers' names were ten columns — a positive column and a negative column each for Monday, Tuesday,

Wednesday, Thursday, and Friday. Each one of us kept his own record. Every time a teacher smiled or said something nice to us, we were to make a mark in the positive column for the day it happened. Or if we got a nasty wisecrack, the mark went in the negative column.

The reason we were spending two weeks counting positive and negative contacts, Miss Cota said, was to "establish norms." She said, "We must have this information before we can know what effect the reinforcing behavior is having later. It's like going on a diet. If you don't know your weight before you begin, you can't tell if the diet's doing any good."

When it came to teacher contacts, Miss Cota had us count everything. Maybe I'd give a correct answer in class and a teacher would say, "Good." That was a positive contact and I was supposed to mark it down on my record sheet. Funny things could happen, though. Once my math teacher, Mrs. Mulhaney, came down the aisle between the desks and I handed her an overdue homework assignment I'd done the night before. She glanced at it and said, "My, this looks nice," so I sneaked a positive contact mark for her in the back of my notebook. But then she added, "But it's late, as usual." So I had to score a negative contact too.

53

Other times it wasn't so easy to decide which column a contact belonged in or if it was any kind of a contact at all. One day Coach was talking to four of us guys in gym class. He said, "You fellows form a line by the wall." Then he looked at me and said, "You too, Roberts." It was his tone of voice that I wasn't sure about. It was almost nasty but not quite. I asked Miss Cota if it was a negative contact. She made me act out before the others exactly what Coach had done and said. Levon and Ernie and Richard and Oscar all said it was negative so that's the way I scored it.

From the first day, Miss Cota made us add our total contacts and then divide by five to get our daily average, then she charted these daily averages on a graph. She guarded that graph like a military secret. She brought it with her to class every afternoon and after she'd entered the day's results, she'd tack it up on the bulletin board till class was over. Afterwards, she packed it in her briefcase and took it with her when she left. She wouldn't risk anyone at school seeing what our project was about — that's how much of a secret it was. As we completed our weekly records, she kept those, too, and nearly threw a conniption once when Ernie forgot and tossed his in the wastebasket.

Even though we wouldn't be reinforcing our teachers till later, Miss Cota started right away teaching us how. The second day she explained how important "small talk" was. "You'll have to get over your shyness about stopping by the teacher's desk to say hello," she said. "When you stop to chat with a teacher, it's a way of saying, 'I like you. I think you're a nice person.' "

"Waste of time," declared Richard.

"Don't you believe it," said Miss Cota. "It's a valuable conversational skill, and it isn't all that hard to learn." She turned to Levon. "Pretend I'm one of your teachers. Say something to me."

Levon didn't want to but Miss Cota insisted. "Come on. Anything. Look me straight in the eye when you say it."

Levon said, "Miss Cota, you part your hair the straightest of anybody ever I see," and Miss Cota laughed till a tear leaked from the corner of her eye. We did a lot of "pretending" like that, for practice. "Role playing," Miss Cota called it. Ernie might pretend to be Coach and I'd practice on him or Levon would pretend to be Mrs. Tatum so Richard could practice. Sometimes it was a real gas.

It's hard to explain what began happening to us in Miss Cota's class. Meeting together every day, we got to know each other and I suppose what happened was we began to relax. We had fun, we really did. The first few days I maintained a low profile for understandable reasons. The chicken thieves were easing up on me and I didn't want to do anything to alter the trend.

But there were times when they wouldn't let me fade into the background. If a question came up about school rules, for instance, they always asked me. (I was the only one who'd read them.) Once Ernie tried to look up "operant" in the dictionary and after we waited ten minutes, Miss Cota made me go help him. After that, when words had to be looked up, I was always the one who did it.

I didn't ask to run the TV equipment but ended up doing that too. It was really neat, what all could be done with it. The TV camera could be hooked directly to the monitor for instant viewing or it could be set on record so it made a videotape to be played back later. If you already knew how to run a plain audio tape recorder, which I did, no problem. All I needed to learn was which buttons to push and how to adjust for focus.

Almost from the first day, Miss Cota made a big thing of teaching us how to smile. You'd have thought everybody knew how to smile, but she proved we were exceptions with our first real videotaped session. She set the camera and the monitor side by side, then one at a time she'd make us sit in a chair in front of them and watch ourselves practice smiling.

Richard was the worst. He never got much better, either, because he wouldn't try. Levon had a hard time too. She was built like a stone wall with a deadpan face to match. She'd gotten in the habit of hiding behind this vacant expression she wore around all the time. She didn't even know what a smile felt like — in her muscles, I mean — and Miss Cota practically had to give her a facial massage to show her.

"You ought to practice smiling at home," Ernie told Levon. "Me, I spent an hour in front of the mirror last night."

Worried, Miss Cota said to Ernie, "You aren't trying these techniques on your parents, are you?"

"Naw! Naw!" Ernie said in a tone of voice that said plain as day he was lying.

"I advise you not to try it," Miss Cota warned him. "You aren't sure what you're doing yet and all you'll do is make a mess."

"All I did at home was practice smiling! No kidding!" Ernie protested. "Nothing wrong with that, is there?"

Ernie's smile had improved and we told him so but Richard said he looked like the Cookie Monster. Richard had a put-down for everything.

Although Miss Cota didn't exactly forbid us to tell our parents, I got the impression she'd just as soon we didn't. I was sorry in a way. Mom would have gotten a charge out of hearing about it. The only trouble with telling Mom was that I couldn't figure out a way to do it without explaining how I happened to be chosen — and I couldn't explain why I was chosen without explaining how I happened to be in Mr. Jarrett's room in the first place — and so on and so on. It was like a frayed sweater — one pulled thread and the whole works would unravel.

Besides learning to smile, we did other things with the TV equipment. We took turns pretending to be a teacher so each of us could practice "small talk." We watched our gestures and facial expressions and listened to the way we sounded.

Most of all, though, the TV equipment taught all of us to pay more attention to the way we dressed. Miss Cota usually got to class before we did. She'd set the camera on record so the tape would pick up each of us as we walked into the room and sat down. It took a few days for us to remember she was doing it.

At first it was really a jolt! When I first came to Rio Verde, I'd been scared spitless of the guff I'd have to take because I was so small. I'd gotten the guff, all right, but the misery I'd had to take from Richard was so much worse by comparison that I didn't even care anymore. I'd gotten so I didn't care about *anything* anymore, least of all my appearance, and on the monitor I came across like Charlie Bucket before he inherited the chocolate factory. After a few days with Miss Cota's TV equipment, though, I remembered to comb my hair more often and keep my shirttail tucked in the way I used to at St. Michael's. I even got Mom to show me how to press a crease in my jeans.

It made a difference with the others too, seeing how they looked. Oscar got himself some clean T-shirts and Ernie cut out some of his stupid clowning around when he found out it wasn't as cool as he thought. Richard didn't take the project very seriously but I noticed his posture improved.

But the biggest change was Levon. She fixed up her hair and began wearing a little jewelry and make-up. Instead of sprawling in a chair like a load of wet laundry, she sat like Diana Ross on a TV talk show. She began to look like Diana Ross too. By the end of the first week, Ernie was walking with her to class and carrying her books.

It wasn't till later that Miss Cota began teaching us the verbal reinforcers we'd be using later with our teachers. "You can smile, of course, and say thanks when there is positive teacher contact. Remember to look them straight in the eye. Then there will also be remarks and comments you can make. You'll have a list of these in your notebooks but you should memorize them."

Ernie said, "Miss Cota, what if a teacher chews us out? What do we do then?"

"Nothing," said Miss Cota. "Don't respond at all if you can help it. Turn away or leave as soon as possible without appearing rude. The same with all negative contacts. That's behavior you want to extinguish." She hadn't given us that word before and she made us say it, "ex-tin-guish."

Hearing her talk about extinguishing undesirable behavior was really interesting to me. The most undesirable behavior I'd ever run across was Richard's shakedown racket, which he had kept up at the rate of one or two mornings a week. One or two mornings was better than five mornings a week, still I thought how nifty it would be if I could extinguish his habit completely.

I stayed after class one day and asked Miss Cota how I should go about extinguishing the behavior of a fellow student on the school grounds who was bullying me. If I'd known then what I found out later, I'd have at least given her a hint that the bully I referred to was a member of our little group and knew as much about reinforcement procedures as I did. But Miss Cota took it for granted the bully was an outsider and she didn't hesitate. "The first rule to remember is to adopt a positive strategy," she said. "Substitute other behaviors for the ones you want to get rid of, but all the time you're doing that, ignore the bullying behavior you want to extinguish."

The next day at noon I got my chance. Mr. Jarrett had organized a basketball game on the outdoor court on the playground. The ball got away from us just as Richard and Ernie came walking across one end of the court. The ball bounced past Richard's shoulder and he caught it. I went toward him with my hands up to catch it and he threw it to me. Like a dope, I smiled at him and said, "Hey, thanks, Richard! It's great when you help out like that."

Shazam! I'd said the magic words but something

went wrong with the formula. Richard did a double take and grabbed me furiously by the front of my shirt. "You little stink!" he snarled. "You try that reinforcing crap on me, I'll slice you up like a hunk of bacon. Where d'you get off, trying to make *me* do what *you* want?"

Then he turned me loose, nearly shoving me down in the process. "All goes to show," he observed bitterly. "I let up collecting from you a couple of mornings and look what happens. Well, get this, kid, holiday's over! And what's more, I'm making up for lost time. You show up in the usual place in the morning, hear? And dues is *double* from now on. One dollar! Every morning! You in a mood to reinforce somebody's behavior, Peewee, you try reinforcin' *that!*"

five

Prince Valiant would have handled it better. He would have extinguished the culprit's undesirable behavior with one stroke of his broadsword and led the villain back to the castle keep with the aid of the best reinforcer of all, chains. My confidence in Miss Cota's project evaporated.

Meanwhile, as far as the wherewithal to pay Richard was concerned, I was up against a blank wall and had to do something about it. I'd already used up the money I'd been saving for Mom's Christmas present. I scrounged a couple more jobs in the neighborhood doing yard work even though I was so strung out from hunger I wasn't sure I could handle it. Before the week was over, I had to do something that nearly killed me; I had to sell the catcher's mitt Dad had given me for my birthday just before he died.

Richard didn't miss a single morning. I was skipping lunch again, regularly, which meant that by the time I got to Miss Cota's class every afternoon, I was beat.

Miss Cota was too preoccupied to notice. Our two weeks of establishing norms were up and it was time to start reinforcing our teachers. I couldn't get excited about it like the others. Just the opposite. Remembering how Richard reacted to Miss Cota's behavior mod techniques, it made me nervous to think what we were in for the first time we tried them on the teachers.

I figured the others could stick their necks out if they wanted to, but not me. The first couple of days of the reinforcing phase, I had a few positive contacts from my teachers, just as I'd always had, but the only reinforcement I tried was smiling, which seemed a darn sight safer. Nobody can hang you for smiling.

I didn't expect any of it to work. When the others began reporting increased positive contacts, I thought they must be hallucinating. So did Miss Cota. All of us had classes together in Mr. Jarrett's room and Ernie and Levon and Richard had some ninth grade classes together. Miss Cota grilled each of us like a police detective, checking up on the others. It was harder to check up on Oscar because he had all remedial classes, or on me because I was the only seventh grader and had classes different from all of them.

It wasn't till the third day that Ernie and Levon made a believer out of me. I watched them go to work on Mr. Jarrett.

To fully appreciate what happened, you have to understand ahead of time that Arnold Jarrett, U.S.M.C. (ret.) was about as responsive as a geode. He was a good teacher but he just wasn't human.

Ernie needed this particular book on Indians for social studies. He made such a loudmouth pest of himself with the other kids in class that finally Mr. Jarrett had to locate it for him. Ernie beamed at Mr. Jarrett, thanked him, and said, "Not many teachers'll go out of their way to do a kid a favor, Mr. Jarrett. It's good, being in your class."

I held my breath waiting for Ernie to get his teeth slapped down his throat for smarting off, but instead Mr. Jarrett's eyes crinkled ever so slightly at the corners! *He thought it was funny!* An hour later, Ernie was trying to erase a problem he'd worked wrong on a page of math homework. His eraser was worn out and all he was doing was shredding the paper. Mr. Jarrett noticed the trouble Ernie was having and handed him his own pencil to use because it had a better eraser. Ernie erased his problem, smiled, and handed back the pencil, gratitude oozing from every pore. "Sure makes me want to work harder when the teacher helps out like that."

"Any time," Mr. Jarrett responded, and gave Ernie a chummy pat on the shoulder!

I nearly fell out of my chair.

Levon wasn't wasting any time, either. Mr. Jarrett showed a film on how to prepare a written report and when Levon couldn't see the screen, Mr. Jarrett asked her if she wanted to move. Levon was right in there, flashing her big Diana Ross smile. "I'm lucky to be in a class where the teacher cares about the kids," she said. Later Mr. Jarrett picked up a piece of chalk she dropped and offered to help her with a punctuation exercise for English. Ernie and Levon had a real thing going and it didn't take Miss Cota to recognize what it was.

Back when we were establishing norms during the first two weeks of the project, the five of us had averaged about eight negative contacts a day to maybe three positive contacts. It varied some but not much. The

Monday we began the behavior mod phase, the pattern changed. That first day our averages came out six negative contacts to four positive contacts. Tuesday we were even-Steven, six to six. Wednesday when we figured the contacts, there were more positives than negatives for the first time — five to three. Miss Cota marked the results on the graph and thumbtacked it up on the bulletin board. We stood around it and stared. It was too good to be true! Miss Cota shook her head in wonder. "I knew all along it would work," she said, "but in *three days?!*"

I gradually became convinced that there might be something to Miss Cota's techniques after all and I began to get with it. From the smile I'd ventured at the beginning, I stepped up the wattage to a smile plus "This is sure a nice class." It worked like a magic elixir. I grew cockier and tried other reinforcers Miss Cota had given us. They worked too. I dreamed up a beaut of my own: "I appreciate it when you build up my self-confidence. You make me want to vindicate your trust in me." This flight of rhetoric elicited a glance of alarm from Mr. Rodriguez, my science teacher. I interpreted it as a warning and toned down my approach to a style more in keeping with my modest character.

Manipulating my teachers was old stuff to me after all those years I'd spent at St. Michael's pretending to be a superbrain. Deceit was the rule I'd lived by — deceit plus the fear that I'd be found out. Miss Cota's behavior mod methods only seemed to me an improved way of accomplishing the same old result, social survival.

Her way was better than mine for a reason I hadn't counted on. In the behavior mod project, I tried so hard to sound sincere saying all those mushy things, I found myself starting to really *be* sincere. I wasn't afraid of being found out because I wasn't hiding much of anything. I got so I truly liked my teachers a lot better and they liked me better. I was still the quietest kid in my classes but I didn't qualify as a loner any longer. Without intending to, I began talking to the other kids instead of answering in monosyllables when they said anything to me. The put-downs about my size dropped off. Both the teachers and the kids respected me! Miss Cota had given me a brand new life and it beat the old one I'd had at St. Michael's by a considerable distance.

We hadn't paid much attention to Miss Cota's progress chart before, but now we couldn't stay away from it. The rest of that first week and through the second, the line showing the positive contacts kept going up and the negative contacts line kept going down.

There had to be a catch somewhere. One day Ernie said, "I don't care what you say, Miss Cota, teachers ain't all that dumb. They got to suspect something's going on."

Miss Cota grinned. "Of course they do! Mr. Podovsky tells me he's been getting remarks about what good work you're all doing in class."

"Sure," agreed Levon. "That's because we *are* doing better."

"I'd question that," Miss Cota said with a firm shake of her head. "You have exactly the same brains you entered school with in September, don't you?"

Levon nodded. "Yeah, but —"

"Your capacity to learn hasn't changed a bit. It's your teachers' attitudes toward you that have changed. They think you're better students now because you've *made* them think so and maybe you've convinced yourselves in the process!"

"They ain't going to like it when they find out what we been up to," said Ernie darkly.

But Miss Cota wasn't worried. "They're reasonable people. The techniques we're using are producing excellent results. How can they deny it?"

70

"Yeah, but Old Lady Tatum —" Levon began.

"Now, now," Miss Cota cut her off. "Mrs. Tatum is a charming, intelligent woman. When the proper time comes, Mrs. Tatum and I will talk this thing over and there'll be no trouble at all. You'll see. Let me worry about Mrs. Tatum," and she bustled us off to more lessons in front of the TV camera.

In spite of Miss Cota's denial, all of us were learning more in our classes and we knew it. Oscar was stuck with the brain of a pachyderm and couldn't get his homework assignments or reports done by himself. For the first time ever since he started school, he got the extra coaching he needed. Teachers helped him. Kids helped him. The librarian helped him. He dropped the happy loser act and actually started learning something on his own for a change. Even with my off-and-on stomach pains, I was making A's and B's on my daily work the way I used to at St. Michael's. Even Richard studied for tests and turned in homework assignments now and then, something he'd never done before.

All of us were getting along better with our teachers but Levon got the most positive contacts. She branched out, you might say. She used verbal reinforcers like the rest of us, but tried other rewards that really meant

71

something to the teachers in terms of assistance. When Mr. Barrows told her she looked nice, she offered to pass out maps for the test he was about to give. One cloudy day when Miss Karl congratulated her on a good grade she made in math, it wasn't sixty seconds before Levon was up at Miss Karl's desk saying, "Miss Karl, it's starting to rain. Want me to go roll up your car windows?" Things like that. Levon's teachers adored her.

Richard was another story. He couldn't get the hang of it. The first time he tried to reinforce Mrs. Tatum, it was a disaster. Mrs. Tatum had asked the class a review question and when Richard gave the right answer, Mrs. Tatum said, "Good, Richard. I see you remember yesterday's lesson," and went ahead with what she was talking to the class about. Anyone else would have let it go, but Richard was determined to reinforce Mrs. Tatum or bust. He interrupted her and said, very loud, "Nice to have a teacher who tells you when you do good," with a sexy leer that suggested the two of them might "do good" together in other ways. Mrs. Tatum told him to keep his smart remarks to himself.

Richard began to suspect the rest of us were cheating in some way. Me, especially. I was getting almost as many positive contacts as Levon and Richard thought I was onto something I wouldn't tell him about. It was ironic that all the time I was paying him fifty cents a day, he joked and kidded around when he met me in the mornings, but now that I was killing myself to pay him a dollar a day, he was really turned off. He was so surly and crabby, you'd have thought I was the one who was shaking him down instead of vice versa.

The yard work jobs took a lot out of me on weekends but I got along better than I thought I would. Mom was gone all day Saturdays working at the store and she never nailed me down about how much I earned. I learned to take along my own equipment, especially our hose from home for watering. It wasn't one of those green plastic drugstore jobs but the big old-fashioned kind that could soak a whole yard in ten minutes and hose down the walks in two. With the nozzle adjusted right, I could demolish a snail at twenty feet, which was a good thing. I needed all the help I could get.

We'd been into the reinforcing phase of the project about three weeks by then. Believe it or not, Ernie and Oscar were turning out to be a couple of really likable guys. I got along swell with them and it made me madder than ever when they showed up with Richard at the Florence Avenue gate every morning. Thanks to Miss Cota, I understood what had happened with the three of them even if Richard didn't understand himself, and I had to bite my tongue to keep from making wisecracks about it.

One morning Mom slept late — she'd been out to a party the night before — and since I had the kitchen to myself before I went to school, I grabbed the opportunity and fixed a sack lunch. At the Florence Avenue gate, I handed over Richard's dollar as usual but this time he wasn't content with just the money. "What you got in the sack, Peewee?" he said.

"Leave me alone," I told him. "You got your money."

"Look, kid," he snapped. "When I ask you a question, I want an answer. What you got in the sack?"

"C'mon, Richard," said Ernie. "Ain't nothing but his lunch."

Ignoring Ernie, Richard snatched the sack out of my hand before I could dodge. When I tried to get it back, he caught me off balance and I ended up on the ground.

"Look like you ain't never gonna learn no manners," he taunted.

While I brushed myself off and picked up my books, Richard reached into the sack and pulled out my sandwich. He unfolded one end of the wax paper and sniffed. "Whew! Baloney! Kid, you don't want to eat pig slop like that!" He threw the sandwich over his shoulder and the way it flew apart, you'd have thought somebody shot it with a .22.

He dug into the sack again and this time brought out my apple. He decided he didn't want that either and gave it to Ernie, who shrugged and began to eat it.

Last in the sack was an egg I'd hard-boiled. It was a tempting missile and Richard looked around for a target. "Wonder if I can hit that post," he said.

"Betcha can't," said Ernie between bites of the apple.

Richard threw the egg at the fencepost by the gate but missed, and the egg squashed on the pavement beyond. There being no more toys in the sack to play with, he wandered off with Oscar.

Ernie hung back. "Too bad you made Richard mad about throwing that basketball," he said. "Gonna be a long time before he forgets it. You shouldn't've tried that psychology stuff on him."

"Why not?" I asked hotly. "He uses that psychology stuff on you and Oscar all the time."

Ernie's eyes widened a moment, then he chuckled. "Man, you sure got crazy ideas."

"It's not a crazy idea, it's the truth." With a nod at the apple in his hand, I said, "There's your reward. He's been reinforcing you with peanuts and candy all along. By now he's got you and Oscar trained to mind him like a couple of seals in a circus act. You watch." I jerked my head toward Richard and Oscar who were about a hundred feet away, walking toward the school building. "In a minute now, Richard's going to call you. And you'll go, too."

"You fulla crap," Ernie said good-naturedly.

"Bet?"

Right on cue, Richard turned and called, "Hey, Ernie! C'mon!"

Before he thought, Ernie called back, "Comin'!" and hurried a few quick steps in Richard's direction.

If I hadn't been so teed off, I'd have died laughing. It was a riot. Ernie stopped and turned, staring at the apple. Shamefaced, he started to look at me but couldn't. He ducked his head and followed Richard.

I knew I'd made my point.

six

All this time, it had been really weird the way Richard and Ernie and Oscar had been casually robbing me every morning, and then every afternoon in Miss Cota's class all four of us pretended it never happened. The morning Richard ruined my lunch marked the end of an era. After that, Ernie never came to the Florence Avenue gate with Richard and a couple of days later, Oscar stopped coming too.

Don't get the wrong idea. The three of them were still together a lot on the school grounds and sat together in Mr. Jarrett's room — at least they did unless Ernie was hanging around Levon. What was finally wearing thin was the pretense that everything was okay between Richard and me. He'd always ridiculed me in a good-natured way — about my size and anything else you care to name — and I'd had it up to here. We traded sarcasms and barbed remarks with more heat than Miss Cota approved of and she called us down fairly often. She learned not to pair us off for role-playing or work in front of the TV camera.

When Richard met me in the mornings, he never did anything physical like roughing me up. Maybe he was afraid of busting his glasses and without them he was blind as a mole. But he talked meaner than ever. Apparently he wanted to make sure I didn't get any ideas about refusing to pay him or squealing on him. He brought up Billy Clark's name again and reminded me about the time my clothes and books got stolen in gym. He let me know in little ways that he knew where I lived, where Mom worked, and what kind of car she drove. Though he never mentioned it, I was certain he still had our housekey and would use it if it suited him.

There wasn't any doubt that he'd been the one who pulled the locker room caper, probably alone. If he was slick enough to get by with a deal like that, right there in school, I was pretty sure he wouldn't get caught if he did other things out of school, such as pour sand in the gas tank of Mom's car or spray-paint dirty words on the front of our house some night while Mom and I were asleep.

Richard didn't need Ernie and Oscar. He could think up plenty of snotty tricks on his own — sometimes right in class. One afternoon the bell had just rung but Miss Cota hadn't come yet. Ernie and Levon were trying to dance and watch themselves on the monitor at the same time. Levon asked me to change the camera so they could videotape themselves. I put my books down on the table but had no sooner gotten the camera fixed when Miss Cota came in to start class.

Meanwhile, behind my back, Richard, the snake, had done something with my books because when I went back to the table they were gone. I asked Richard what he did with my books.

He put on a phony-innocent act that wouldn't have fooled a three-year-old. "What books? I don't know nothing about no books!"

Miss Cota glared at him. "Where are Varnell's books, Richard?" she snapped.

Meanwhile Levon — who is the world's champion second-guesser — had already gone to look out the window. "Varnell, your notebook's blue, right?" she said. "Richard done throwed your books out the window."

It wasn't an enormously big deal since our classroom was on the first floor and from the window it was only a six-foot drop to the ground. It was the pettiness of it that made me so mad. I mean, how gross can you get?

I held my temper and without a word, I started out the door to go get my books.

"Sit down, Varnell," Miss Cota commanded. "Richard is the one who dropped your books out the window so he's the one who'll go get them."

"He'll tear them up," I said.

"He won't tear them up," she insisted, and she repeated her order to Richard to go get my books. "Move!" she barked at him.

The way Richard waltzed out of the room, you'd have thought she'd pinned a medal on him.

As soon as he was gone, Levon said, "Miss Cota, you ought to make Richard stop deviling Varnell. He does it all the time."

I stared. It was the first time in my life I'd ever heard a black person taking up for a honky. I was grateful to Levon even though I knew what she said wouldn't do any good.

81

Miss Cota gazed sternly at Levon and then, sure enough, she went into her catechism routine. "Richard displays undesirable behavior, right?" she asked Levon.

"Yeah," Levon replied, unimpressed.

"Isn't that what we've been working on in this project, changing undesirable behavior?"

"Yeah."

"And how do we do it?"

"We extinguish undesirable behavior by ignoring it at the same time we establish desirable behavior by reinforcing it," Levon quoted, letter perfect.

"So there you are." As far as Miss Cota was concerned, the matter was closed.

"Yeah, but that system don't work for everybody," Levon persisted.

It was heresy but Miss Cota kept her cool. "Yes, Levon, it works for everybody. You're right about Richard, though," she admitted. "In the beginning, I should have paid attention and handled the problem better."

About that time, Richard ambled back with the books and slung them down on the table in front of me. I checked them.

"My math homework assignment's gone," I notified Miss Cota.

"He's lying!" Richard cried with the same phony innocence as before. "He's trying to get me in trouble!"

Levon's harsh voice cut the air. "Give him his math assignment, Richard." She wasn't smiling.

Ernie added gravely, "Give it to him, Richard. Won't do you no good, you haven't got the same teacher for math. All you'll do is throw it away."

Grinning and shaking his head in mock resignation, Richard took a folded sheet of notebook paper from his pocket and threw it across the table at me.

Miss Cota glared at him. "Let's not have any more of *that!*" she barked, and we started class as usual.

I tried to forget about it but couldn't. I'd had other clashes with Richard but this one was different. For the first time, a friend of Richard's and the teacher herself had turned against him. Why wasn't he resentful? Levon had said Miss Cota's system of rewarding desirable behavior didn't work for everybody. I decided Levon must know something about Richard I didn't know, having been acquainted with him in school longer than I had. Next day at noon I went to find Levon.

We located a vacant tree and sat down on the grass. Levon was still a little fed up about Miss Cota. "Scientific!" Levon said, disgusted. "Where she get off with that scientific stuff? New kind of charm school is what she's running. You ever think you'd end up in a charm school?"

"No."

"That's all it is. Teach you how to look better, act better, help you get what you want."

"You got what you want?" I asked Levon.

"You crazy? Sure I got what I want! Not just me, all of us! Kids not ugly to us like they used to be. Teachers sweet as pie. Good grades for a change." She pulled a blade of grass. "Why? You ain't got what you want?"

I shook my head.

Thoughtfully, she split the blade of grass down the middle. "You got trouble with Richard." I noticed it wasn't a question. Ernie would have told her. About the protection racket, about Billy Clark — all of it, probably.

"Richard, he's not like the rest of us," Levon mused. "Now my mama's no saint, goodness knows, still she takes up for me in a jam, know what I mean? But Richard, his mama and daddy run off and left him when he was a baby. Maybe you didn't know that."

I shook my head.

"Been raised by this aunt he's got. Only time she

pays any attention to him is when she comes home drunk and near about whips him to death. Richard ain't never had nobody be nice to him. Nobody. Scares him, somebody trying to be friendly."

Scares him? Richard Hogarth, scared? And then I remember the way he turned on me that day with the basketball, like a cornered diamondback. It didn't make sense. "You know what he really likes?" I said to Levon. "What he really likes is when everybody talks mean to him. I don't get it."

"Business about your books?"

"Yeah. He threw my books out the window and we all jumped on him. And he liked it!"

"Sure, that's Richard." Levon pulled another blade of grass and split it down the middle. "See, Richard got all this fight bottled up inside. Can't help it if some of it spew out sometimes, get him in trouble. Scares him, like I said. Only time he feels safe is when he got people around him tough enough to fight back. That way he can't hurt 'em."

"Miss Cota's tough," I said.

"Sure, she's tough. You notice she's about the only teacher Richard respects, too." She paused before she went on. "Tell you something else. Miss Cota, maybe she carry all that book stuff around in her head but deep down she knows well as I do won't none of that reinforcing junk work on Richard. She uses it on us all the time — you and me and Ernie and Oscar. Works like a charm. But you ain't seen her use it on Richard. Not once."

Across the school grounds the bell rang, shrilling the air. Levon gathered her books and stood. "Anybody want to keep Richard in line need to figure out a good put-down for him every day," she said. "Make him do right. Stand up to him."

That afternoon I was so preoccupied I forgot to reinforce Miss Mulhaney or Mr. Barrows. Levon had put into words what I'd been too chicken to admit on my own. If I was ever to get out of the trap Richard Hogarth had forced me into, I'd have to confront him myself. I could count on the others for moral support but the tough part was up to me.

That night I lay awake trying to figure out ways to avoid making the same mistakes Billy Clark did. If a quarrel between Richard and me ended up in Mr. Podovsky's office, would Ernie and Oscar tell what they knew? I was certain they wouldn't.

At 2 A.M., I was still mentally rehearsing what I would say to Richard next morning. Once I got up to find judo defense strategies in this book I had. I even practiced a few of them. Staying hungry so much of the time, my physical endurance was shot but I still had strength enough for a few quick licks.

I was up and down most of the night. Finally Mom called from her room for Pete's sake to stop it, whatever I was doing, and go to sleep.

I catnapped till dawn. By the time daylight appeared, the last of my courage ebbed into the dark corners of the room. "Admit it, Roberts," I said to myself. "You don't have the guts to fight Richard Hogarth and you know it. You are nothing but a cowardly, pusillanimous, yellow-livered toad!"

I choked down breakfast and walked the six blocks to school with Richard's four quarters in my pocket and despair in my heart. For the first time, I tried to imagine what it would be like — what it would *really* be like — to keep Richard Hogarth supplied with pocket money for the rest of the school year and probably even after that. Next year Richard would graduate to senior high, but so what? Other kids often returned to Rio Verde for visits and there was no reason why Richard couldn't do the same.

To remind myself of what lay ahead, with each block I walked I remembered more of what I'd had to put up with from Richard Hogarth for the past two months. The more grievances and injustices I remembered, the madder I got. And the madder I got, the faster I walked and the more easily certain facts began to fall into place. Maybe I had a chance after all.

By the time I got to school, I was running.

seven

Richard didn't come to meet me that morning, I went to meet him. He was over by the Prince Road fence, watching some ninth grade kids playing softball. Oscar and Ernie were with him, and that was fine with me. There was a better chance it would be a fair fight if they were there than if they weren't.

Richard saw me coming. "Got the money you owe me, Peewee?"

I squared off in front of him and called him a string of names it would be embarrassing to repeat. Kids began to gather, just as I'd hoped they would. Win or lose, I'd have witnesses.

"I've got my money, all right," I told Richard, "but

I don't owe you a dime of it! You want to collect any money off of me, you'll have to take it away from me!"

The smile left Richard's face. "Now that ain't nice, acting like that, Peewee. You asking for trouble."

"Name's Varnell Roberts, not Peewee," I went on, good and loud so everyone could hear. "Ever since you started your protection racket with me in September, you've been talking about the trouble I'm supposed to get into. You keep threatening to steal all my clothes again like you did in gym class or you're going to run me out of school like you did Billy Clark last year. You've been stealing money from me every day and I've been a sucker to put up with it. But no more. I'm through!"

He directed a pitying smile at me. "Listen to the crazy kid! I ain't stole a cent from you, Peewee. You been sitting out in the sun too long. Brain's gone soft."

"My brain's gone soft all right. Nobody but a soft-headed jerk would keep paying you off every morning the way I have!"

"You claim I been collecting this money from you," Richard challenged. "Let's see you prove it!"

"There are two people who can prove it," I said, being careful not to look at Ernie or Oscar. "You know who they are as well as I do. You've made suckers of

91

them just like you made a sucker out of me. They have to decide for themselves if they want to keep covering for you or not. But that's their business. Right now, you and I are the ones with the score to settle. If you don't want those glasses of yours to get busted, you better take 'em off!"

Pained, Richard turned away. "Buzz off, kid. You bore me."

I shifted so that once again I stood in front of him. "Are you going to fight me or not?"

" 'S matter, Richard, you chicken or something?" yelled someone in the crowd.

"Chicken, hell!" Richard blazed back. "I ain't fighting a gnat like him!"

"Why not?" I challenged. "You don't mind running a shakedown racket with gnats like Billy Clark and me for victims. Now all of a sudden you've changed your mind and don't want to fight somebody smaller than you. I'll tell you something, mister, you really *are* chicken!"

Richard snapped, "That does it! Kid, you pushed me far enough. Oscar, show this runt who's boss around here."

But Oscar just stood there, gazing first at me and then at Richard.

92

Richard yelled at him. "Oscar! I'm talking to you! Straighten this kid out!"

"I ain't got nothing against Varnell," Oscar said softly.

Onlookers in the circle around us began to hoot and jeer. Kids were crowded around ten deep by now and more coming all the time.

Through gritted teeth, Richard snarled at Oscar, "I didn't ask you what you got against him. I told you, *lean on him!*"

"Lean on him yourself," Ernie intervened mildly. "You ain't so blind without them glasses you need Oscar and me to back you up. Might do you good to get a little dusty yourself for a change."

It was the break I'd hoped for. Richard was half a head taller than me but I was quicker. In a fair fight, I might even stand a chance of whipping him if it didn't go on too long.

But Richard turned on Ernie, "Some friends I got! This is the way you and Oscar pay me back after all I done for you!"

And then from out of nowhere, Levon appeared, standing at my elbow and closing the hostile circle around Richard.

"You too?" Richard sneered bitterly. "It figures."

He turned to me. "Ain't given up yet, trying to change my behavior, have you, Peewee? Sneaked around behind my back. Even got Levon lined up on your side. Well, I got a trick or two I can play too, don't forget." He surveyed the four of us, one by one. "Yes, sir. I can fix everything just fine." He shoved his way through the bystanders and marched across the school grounds to the main building just as Old Everready, the cop, came shouldering his way through the crowd from the opposite direction yelling, "Break it up! Break it up!"

A moment later the special ed bell rang and we had to go in to Mr. Jarrett's homeroom. Richard was already there, hunched over a magazine at the reading table and carefully ignoring everyone. Later we went to our regular classes and I didn't see Richard again all morning.

Richard wasn't the type to cave in over a little name-calling and I knew it. Still, I had my own money to buy my own lunch for a change and I thought I'd better enjoy my freedom while I could. I went through the cafeteria line with Ernie and Levon — some kids who'd seen the skirmish with Richard that morning let us in ahead of them — and the three of us ate together.

As soon as we sat down, Levon announced, "Something's wrong." It seemed that Mrs. Tatum had come to see Levon's sewing class teacher and talked to her about fifteen minutes.

Ernie was interested right away. "Mrs. Tatum came to see Coach in gym, too. What you reckon she's up to?"

"Something about the project, I bet," said Levon. "All the time Mrs. Tatum was in sewing class, Mrs. Crawford kept looking at me. Afterwards she acted like she was mad about something. Didn't get a positive contact out of her all period."

Levon asked me if I'd seen Mrs. Tatum that morning but I hadn't.

A few minutes later, Coach walked past the table where we were eating. Ernie had been getting along great with Coach but when Ernie hailed him, Coach stared briefly in our direction, then pointedly turned his back and struck up a conversation with some other kids.

"Richard's blabbed about the project," Levon declared flatly.

From the beginning, Miss Cota had made a big thing of keeping the project secret, and we hadn't questioned it. If word had leaked out during those first days and the teachers had made Mr. Podovsky stop it, we would have missed a lot. But not now. We'd learned what we were supposed to and proved what we were supposed to. The project had only a final week to run before it was over. Where was the damage?

Levon and Ernie and I spent the rest of noon period talking it over. We decided that Miss Cota and Mr. Podovsky stood to get hurt worse than we did. We couldn't figure out why Richard would tip anyone off about the project unless it was for the same reason he dropped my books out the window — just for the fun of causing trouble.

After lunch we went to Miss Cota's class wondering what would happen now. Richard wasn't there and neither was Miss Cota. Ten minutes later, Miss Cota came in. But where was Richard? I was uneasy.

Miss Cota told us exactly what we expected her to. She was late because Mr. Podovsky had stopped her in the hall to tell her the secret about the project was out. She'd tried to laugh it off but apparently Mrs. Tatum had gotten the teachers too worked up for it to be a laughing matter. We could tell Miss Cota was worried.

"How'd Mrs. Tatum find out?" Ernie asked.

"Mr. Podovsky said some notes accidentally fell out of one of your notebooks and Mrs. Tatum found them," Miss Cota said.

" 'Accidentally fell out'?" Levon raised a skeptical eyebrow. "Planted in Mrs. Tatum's room for her to find — that's more likely what you mean."

Miss Cota started. "Who would —?" She searched our faces. "By Richard you mean? Why would Richard do a thing like that?" She shook her head, dismissing the idea. "Mr. Podovsky didn't say Mrs. Tatum found them in her room. For all I know, she might have found them in the hall — anywhere. Where is Richard, by the way?"

"He was in Mrs. Tatum's room for science first period," Levon answered pointedly.

Oscar stirred. "He was in Miss Karl's room for math just before noon. I was in there making up a test. Mrs. Tatum came in and they talked a long time. Afterwards, Miss Karl said she wanted to talk to Richard when class was over. But Richard didn't stay. Last I saw of him, he was headed off across the school grounds."

My uneasiness grew to alarm. "Which way?"

"Florence Avenue gate," Oscar said.

"Did he say where he was going?" I asked.

97

"Said he had to run an errand."

Miss Cota was preoccupied and wasn't listening. "Maybe he got sick and went home," she murmured.

But Richard hadn't gotten sick and gone home. Suddenly I knew why he'd leaked the secret of the project. When I realized how much time I'd let slip by, I caught my breath. I didn't have time to explain or argue — not now. I asked Miss Cota to be excused and didn't say what for. I walked down the hall, out the side entrance of the building, and broke into a dead run for the Florence Avenue gate and home.

I was still a block away when I saw him. He'd warned me, "Ask what happened to Billy Clark." I'd asked, all right, but I hadn't listened carefully enough to the answer. When I spotted Richard walking quickly along the sidewalk, checking house numbers and carrying a five-gallon can, I didn't wonder what was in it. I knew.

I stopped in my tracks, half-hidden by an oleander hedge that extended over the sidewalk. As Richard came even with our house, he paused and glanced up and down the street but didn't see me. As soon as he satisfied himself that no one was around, he darted into the driveway beside our house.

The bungalow Mom and I live in is California

stucco with pyracantha growing over the porch. Attached to one side of the house is a single-car garage that Mom has never once used for the car. We've always used it for storage instead. It has a rickety wooden door that slides up, with a hasp and lock so flimsy the wind blew it off once.

I ran the last block to our house. When I got even with the garage, the lock was lying on the grass by the driveway but Richard was nowhere in sight. Apparently he'd gone inside the garage and pulled down the sliding door so he couldn't be seen from the street.

Running that last block, I realized that once Richard started a fire in the garage, there might not be anything anyone could do to save it. All the houses in our block are tinderboxes built during the Depression with the cheapest materials possible. I tried to remember what I'd done with the garden hose last time I'd used it. As quietly as I could, I skirted the driveway to the side yard and found the hose coiled up under the spigot where I'd left it the Saturday before.

From the garage, I could hear a gurgling sound and footsteps shuffling across the cement floor. I flipped out the hose to its full length, turned on the faucet as far as it would go, and gave the garage door a heave that sent it sailing up on its tracks. And then the smell hit me — gasoline!

Richard hardly had time to turn around. He was pouring out the last drops from the five-gallon can when I nailed him in the face with a jet of water. The effect was like buckshot. His glasses flew off and landed somewhere on the floor behind him. Surprise plus the overpowering force of the water threw him off balance. He dropped the can and started to swear, fighting the water.

I doused him good. If there were any matches on him anywhere, I wanted to make sure they'd be too wet to strike.

Richard lunged at me, trying to dart past the tumbling, sledgehammer blows from the stream of water I kept trained on his face. He covered his head with his arms and retreated, then grabbed a little table Mom had stored out there and tried to use it as a shield. It was too small to help much. Water ricocheted from wall to wall of the garage and soon everything was dripping, even the rafters. If there had been any danger of fire before, there wasn't now.

And then Richard surprised me. Maybe the fumes had made him so dizzy he lost his balance. Maybe he was disoriented without his glasses. With his back to the jet of water, he slid to the floor, pulled his knees to his chest, and sat curled in a ball, head down, without moving at all. It was a gesture of defeat and it came to me, grimly, that I understood the feeling.

I turned the hose away then, and moved to one side of the garage door. Richard turned cautiously and peered at me.

"Get out," I told him.

He groped on the floor for his glasses. One lens was gone but he put them on anyway, stood up, and stumbled past me to the driveway. With his head down and his dripping clothes staining a dark trail behind him on the sidewalk, he turned down the street toward school.

Mom wasn't due home from work till 4:30 which was a good thing because there were some loose ends I had to attend to. I went inside and telephoned Mr. Podovsky at school. It took me awhile to convince the secretary I needed to talk to him personally and a much longer time after that to explain to Mr. Podovsky what had happened and why.

"Don't touch anything in the garage till the police come and fill out a report," he said.

It's a good thing he reminded me because I'm not sure I'd have thought to call the cops. When they came, I had to tell all over again what I'd told Mr. Podovsky. They were there nearly an hour talking to me and going over the garage. When they left, they took the empty gasoline can — which I hadn't touched — and the slivers from Richard's broken glasses that they found on the floor.

Mom wasn't due home for another four hours yet. I hooked up an electric fan in the garage to air the place out and moved most of the water-soaked stuff to the back yard where it could dry in the afternoon sun. It was still there when Mom came home just after dark. I had the porch floodlight on and was moving some of it back to the garage and the rest to the back porch for the night.

Mom isn't the kind that weeps when things go wrong. I thought she was going to have a heart attack instead. When she saw the mess, she stared. Then she sat down (before she fell down) and listened without interrupting while I told the same story over again for the third time that day. (I was getting good at it.) The version I told Mom was longer, though, because in addition to the story about Richard, I told her about

Project Behavior Mod and even dug up ancient history and confessed about fooling the teachers at St. Michael's. It was certainly a relief, being able to tell her.

Afterwards she hugged me — hard — and we hurried to move the rest of the garage things under cover before bedtime. In the middle of shoving cartons and furniture around, she straightened and looked at me. It startled both of us to realize our eyes were on the same level. I'd been so preoccupied with my other problems I'd forgotten to worry about my size; you might say I grew up behind my back.

Mom was impressed. "Varnell Roberts!" she said with a smile that melted my insides, "you aren't a little boy any longer!" There was a quaver in her voice that I'd never heard before. To keep from bawling and making her out a liar on the spot, I looked the other way and patted her on the shoulder in what I hoped was a manly way. My mom is a living doll.

I didn't know what to expect at school next day. Levon, Oscar, Ernie and I got together on the playground before the bell and I told them about Richard and the garage and the cops coming. Kids kept staring at us. I guess the news about the project traveled pretty fast.

The bell rang and we no sooner got inside Mr. Jarrett's door before he told us Mr. Podovsky wanted to see us right away. Mrs. Tatum had gotten to Mr. Jarrett too, because he'd really changed. He was so cold and formal you could've chipped him up for a Sno-Cone.

We had to wait while Mr. Podovsky finished policing the hall and getting the school day started. He called us in one at a time to grill us about Richard. He grilled me less than the others because I'd already told him all I knew over the phone.

"The juvenile authorities have picked up Richard," he told me.

I nodded.

"You'll be needed later to testify in court."

I didn't mind testifying but I hoped Mom would be able to get off work and go with me. Even though I was no longer a little boy I could stand some moral support.

I went to my morning classes and you'd have thought I left my face at home the way the teachers did double takes. (I didn't reinforce anybody.) But the surprise of the day was waiting for us in Miss Cota's classroom after lunch.

None of us knew the man sitting at the table with

105

Miss Cota. He looked like Santa Claus in a Brooks Brothers suit but he turned out to be the superintendent of the school system, Dr. Wheeler.

"Dr. Wheeler has a conference with the teachers scheduled for later this afternoon," Miss Cota explained. "Since he was coming to Rio Verde anyway, I thought his trip should include a meeting with you."

Dr. Wheeler struggled out of his chair and extended his pudgy hand to each of us in turn. He didn't bust out in any ho-ho-hos but he came close. His eyes crinkled merrily and he chirped, "These are the mischief-makers, are they? My! My! They don't look at all evil or sinister, do they, Miss Cota?"

Miss Cota arched an eyebrow in disdain. "Quite a few of the teachers seem to think they are." As a grim afterthought, she added, "And I must say, Richard didn't help our image any along that line."

We all sat down and Levon asked Miss Cota, "Will Richard being gone make any difference about the project? We'll finish it, won't we?"

Miss Cota shook her head. "That's one reason I wanted Dr. Wheeler to be with us today. This is the last time we'll meet together. Mr. Podovsky and I talked it over and decided it would probably be just as well if we terminated the experiment. After all the excitement, any data you gathered this last week wouldn't be valid anyway."

"Teachers are pretty hot about it, ain't they?" Ernie asked.

"They shouldn't be hot about it!" Miss Cota declared. "They should be proud that you've made such fine progress!"

Dr. Wheeler chuckled comfortably. " They'll come to see that, Isabel. Don't worry. Mike asked for evaluations from each of them, remember. That will force them to do a little objective thinking, right there. Just now, their professional pride is hurt."

"But the experiment worked!" Miss Cota said.

"Of course, it worked," said Dr. Wheeler. "That's what makes the situation all the more humiliating for them. As a professional group, teachers probably know more about these techniques and are in a better position to practice them than any other you could name except psychologists themselves. To have a group of children use their own weapons against them, and use them successfully — ah, that takes getting used to."

"You mean teachers know about reinforcing and all that?" Levon asked, incredulous.

"They certainly *should* know," Dr. Wheeler said. "In the teaching profession, these techniques are looked upon as a valuable way to help children succeed in their school work. Every teacher training program in the country includes them. In fact, to my way of thinking, the astounding thing about Miss Cota's project was not that the principles worked as well as they did — it's common knowledge that they work — but that so many trained teachers failed to recognize what was happening! It's that aspect that made the whole thing a little scary for them."

"Why scary?" I asked. "Because they didn't want to like us but they ended up liking us anyway?"

"Mm. You could put it that way, I suppose," said Dr. Wheeler. He tilted his chair back on two legs and steepled his fingers together over his round little belly, thinking. "Power. Yes, that's it. Power. You demonstrated your power over your teachers and you've frightened them. The same way hypnotism used to frighten people. You're familiar with the technique of hypnotism, of course —?"

He looked about, surveying us. We nodded.

"— the droning voice, the staring eye. Is hypnotism a dangerous weapon that one person can use against another? We all know it isn't. Still we have to remember that when hypnotism was first discovered a hundred and fifty years ago, everyone thought it was very dangerous. Dr. Mesmer, the Austrian who discovered it, was forced to terminate his practice in Paris because everyone was so afraid of him and this strange power he had."

"*Afraid* of him!" Ernie chortled. "My little sister got off on a hypnotism kick last year. She learned about it on TV. Tried to hypnotize the cat."

"How old is your sister?"

"Six."

"There, you see?" Dr. Wheeler let his chair down with a bang. "Nowadays, hypnotism is a parlor stunt, mostly. But not entirely. It's used today in clinical situations. Patients go to professional hypnotists for help in giving up smoking, for example, or losing weight. In the same way, there are clinics that specialize in techniques such as these you've been using in your experiment. People go there who want their behavior changed in some way. Perhaps Miss Cota told you that."

Dr. Wheeler was so wound up I hoped we could keep him talking all period. I had some questions I wanted to ask him. But without warning he glanced at the clock and jumped to his feet. "Oh, my! I'm afraid I'm late. I promised to go over your statistics with Mr. Podovsky." His eyes crinkled again. "Boning up for the meeting with the teachers, you know." He shook hands all around and popped out of the room, leaving a vacuum behind.

Finally Miss Cota roused herself and we finished our last teacher contact tabulation, then sat around speculating about Richard. Miss Cota was more depressed than I'd ever seen her. She'd hoped our group would be a pilot class that would provide a pattern for training other groups and maybe she felt all her work had been for nothing. We tried to cheer her up but the attempt was a failure.

We'd all have hated a big parting scene with Miss Cota. It would've been pointless since we knew we'd be seeing her around school just as we always had before. What sobered all of us was that we'd passed a milestone and none of us would ever be the same again. Miss Cota had helped us turn our lives around, and it's hard to put your finger on the kind of gratitude you feel when someone does you a good turn like that.

Just before the bell, I said, "Miss Cota, thanks for all you did for us." Tears welled up in Levon's eyes and she kissed Miss Cota on the cheek. Miss Cota shook hands with Ernie and Oscar and me and the last thing we saw of her, she was racing off down the hall so we wouldn't see her cry.

epilogue

I testified at Richard's juvenile court trial (Mom went) and so did Ernie and Oscar. They told the truth too. Mr. Podovsky told us that the day Richard was arrested, his aunt had kicked him out and wouldn't have anything more to do with him. He served a month at the reformatory for extortion and attempted arson and soon after Christmas was released to work out the rest of his sentence, which was to get a job and pay me back. (It was a nice surprise because I never expected to see any of that money again.) Richard wasn't living with his aunt in the Rio Verde district anymore but fifteen miles away in a foster home with a foster father even tougher than Mr. Jarrett. Mr. Podovsky said Richard was even doing okay at his new school.

111

The biggest surprise, though, was Mr. Podovsky. On the same day I was elected spring term president of Mr. Jarrett's homeroom, Mr. Podovsky called Ernie, Levon, Oscar and me into his office one by one and re-scheduled us back into regular classes. I was very glad to swap being president of Mr. Jarrett's homeroom for getting back in my regular classes but I couldn't under-stand why Mr. Podovsky had suddenly changed his mind after the teachers had thrown such fits.

"The teachers decided the project was worthwhile after all," he said. "They say you kids were the ones who did the changing, not them." It didn't strike me as an especially monumental discovery.

Later, just before I left to go back to class, he gave me a puzzled look and said, "Do you think you changed? Because of the project, I mean?"

Was he kidding? "Yes," I said.

"Why?" he asked. "I mean, why do you think this change came about? What caused it?"

I shrugged. "The TV equipment — having a chance to see how we looked to other people and practicing looking better. And Miss Cota. She taught us how important it is to level with people and let them know when we really appreciate what they do." I hesitated.

"Is that all?"

I was thinking of Levon and Ernie and how they'd helped me in so many little ways. And how all three of us had helped Oscar. And of course, there was Richard. If the others hadn't gone to bat for me when I jumped him, today I'd be a starved skeleton with a busted head and Richard would be just as mean as ever. He wouldn't have changed a bit. The way things were, at least now maybe he had a chance.

I didn't think Mr. Podovsky was going to like what I was about to say, but to keep the record straight, I said it anyway.

"Maybe —" I said to Mrs. Podovsky, "— maybe as much as anything else, we changed each other."

Though the characters and central plot of VARNELL ROBERTS, SUPER-PIGEON are fictitious, the main elements of the story are based on an actual project undertaken in a junior high school at Visalia, California, and reported in *Psychology Today*, March, 1974. ("Little Brother Is Changing You," by Farnum Gray, Paul S. Graubard, and Harry Rosenberg.)

Genevieve Gray